HURRICANE

DAVID WIESNER

ANDERSEN PRESS

"I can't find Hannibal anywhere, Mum," David said. "I thought he'd be home when we got back from the shops."

"I'm sure Hannibal is all right," Mum answered. "Cats know more about storms than people do. But if it will make you feel better, why don't you and George look for him while I put the shopping away. Don't go too far from the house, though. Your father will help you look as soon as he's finished securing everything in the garden."

HURRICANE

For Carol, George, Barbara and Pat

First published in Great Britain in 2017 by Andersen Press Ltd.,
20 Vauxhall Bridge Road, London, SW1V 2SA.
Published by special arrangement with Clarion Books,
an imprint of Houghton Mifflin Harcourt Publishing Company,
and Rights People, London.

10 9 8 7 6 5 4 3 2 1

British Library Cataloguing in Publication Data available.

ISBN 978-1-78344-577-6

TOMAT
CAT FOOD

236

"There he is!" David exclaimed. He and George peered through the gaps between the strips of tape they had put on the storm door. A thoroughly wet Hannibal peered indignantly back at them.

"Let's get him inside before the wind blows him away," George said.

"Could the wind really be strong enough to blow Hannibal away?" David asked.

"Well, the radio said we could expect 'sustained winds of fifty miles per hour, gusting to ninety' any time now, and the hurricane is still fifty miles off the coast. Look at the leaves out there! It looks like a green blizzard!" George answered.

David listened to the walls of the house creaking against the wind. "If it's like this now, what is it going to be like when the hurricane hits?"

Suddenly the lights went out.

"Nobody panic," their dad called from the kitchen. "The electric lines must be down. Hang in there, boys. We're on our way with torches and candles."

They had supper by the fireplace that evening. It felt safe with everybody together, even though there were creaks and groans and sometimes great roaring sounds coming from outside. The hurricane was in full force.

David and George took a hurricane lamp to bed with them. The storm had begun to ease.

"Maybe the eye is passing over us," George said. "I'd like to be in one of those weather planes, the ones that fly into the eye of the hurricane where it's all calm and peaceful."

"Yeah," David said, though he wasn't so certain he'd like to fly into a hurricane. "I wonder where the birds are now, and the squirrels."

"I bet the squirrels are holed up in their trees, but I've read about birds being blown thousands and thousands of miles, maybe even clear across the Atlantic," George said.

"Do you think anything awful has happened outside?" David asked.

"Who knows? We'll see tomorrow," George replied.

The next morning, only one elm tree was standing near the corner of the garden. The day before there had been two. The fallen tree was lying across the neighbour's lawn.

"Look at that!" David said. "It could have hit Mr Wilbur's house, and we didn't even hear it fall!"

"Wow! This is great," George said. They circled the tree. "It looks like a sleeping giant."

"Look at those big limbs and branches! It's like a jungle. Let's play safari. We've never had a jungle to play safari in before." David didn't wait for an answer. He was already climbing the fallen tree.

David fearlessly led the expedition into the very heart of the jungle,

stalking the mighty leopard.

That afternoon they sailed the seven seas with George at the helm,

while David searched the horizon for pirate ships.

All the next day and the day after that, they journeyed to the stars and beyond.

milk
Sunnyside
Farms
milk
milk
Sunnyside
Farms

Sometimes, they just sat and enjoyed the view. The tree was a private place, big enough for secret dreams, small enough for shared adventure.

"What'll we do this afternoon?" George asked.

"I don't care," David answered. "It just feels good being here."

Then it happened. They woke one morning to an ear-splitting roar, and the sight of men advancing on the tree with chainsaws.

JOHNS
SHRUBS

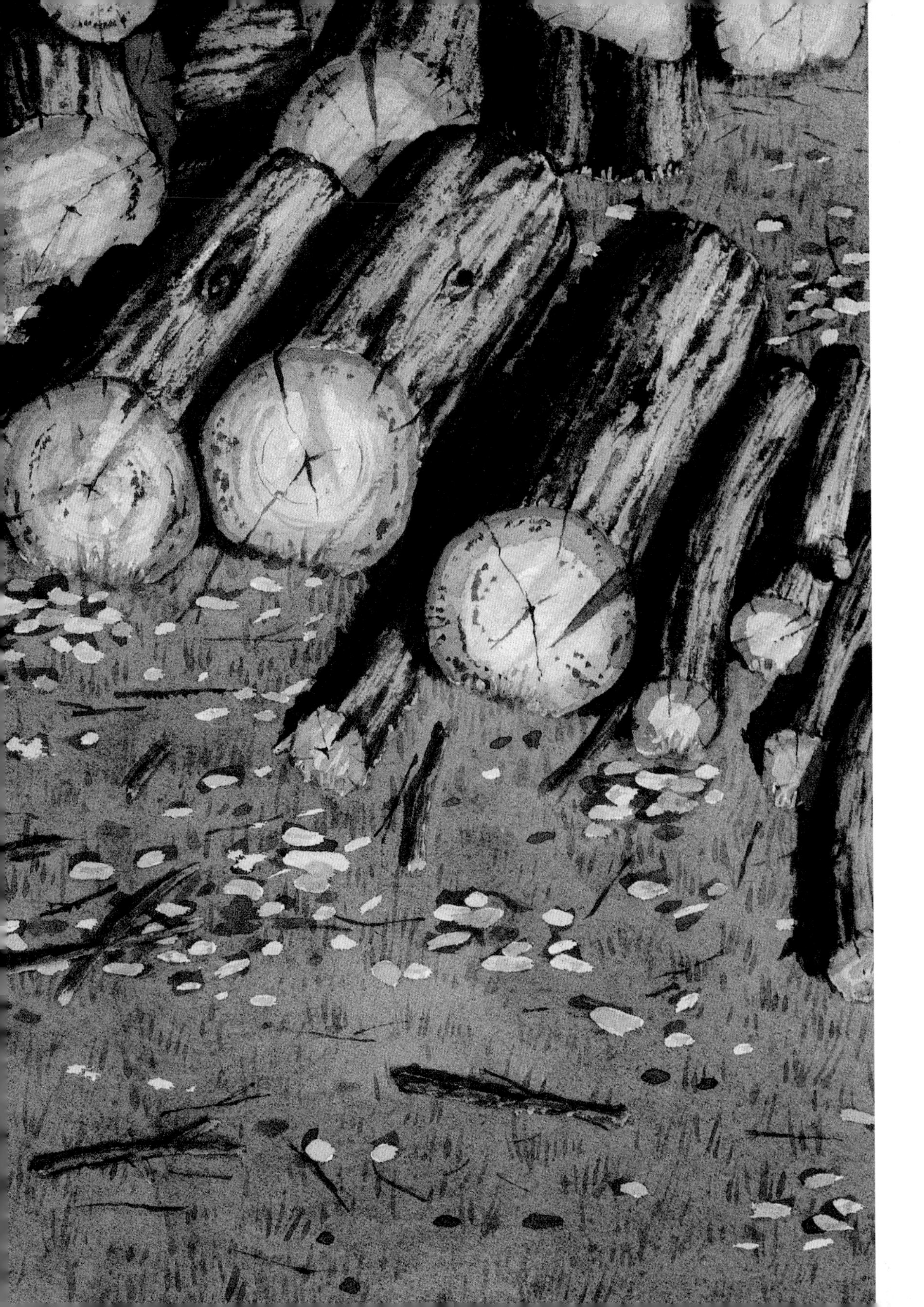

"How could they do this?" David asked. "It's our tree."

"It's our tree, but it's in Mr Wilbur's garden. I suppose that's how they could do it."

"But they didn't even tell us," David said, feeling as miserable as he had ever felt in his life.

"It was a great tree," said George.

"Yeah," David agreed. "A great tree."

David and George spent the rest of the day sitting under the surviving elm, watching the men haul away their tree. In the late afternoon, the sky grew dark and thunder rumbled in the distance.

"Hey, boys," Dad called, "there's going to be a storm. The wind's picking up. Come inside before it starts to rain."

David and George looked up at the old elm.

"This is a great tree, too," David said.

"Yeah," George agreed. "And if it fell, it would land in our garden."